Boy, is *she* mean!

Alex grabbed Janie's arm. "Look," she whispered. "There's Alexandria! See? Over there. That's the mean girl I was telling you about!"

"Did she really throw your towel in the water?" Janie whispered back.

"Yeah," Alex exclaimed. "And she pushed me in the water the first day of swim team practice!"

"Boy, what a creep!" Janie exploded. They continued staring at Alexandria. "I thought someone that mean would be ugly," Janie finally said. "But she's pretty!"

The ALEX Series
by Nancy Simpson Levene

- Shoelaces and Brussels Sprouts
- French Fry Forgiveness
- Hot Chocolate Friendship
- Peanut Butter and Jelly Secrets
- Mint Cookie Miracles
- Cherry Cola Champions
- The Salty Scarecrow Solution
- Peach Pit Popularity
- T-Bone Trouble
- Grapefruit Basket Upset
- Apple Turnover Treasure
- Crocodile Meatloaf
- Chocolate Chips and Trumpet Tricks
  —an Alex Devotional

French Fry Forgiveness

Nancy Simpson Levene

Chariot Books™ is an imprint of
David C. Cook Publishing Co.
David C. Cook Publishing Co., Elgin, Illinois 60120
David C. Cook Publishing Co., Weston, Ontario
Nova Distribution Ltd., Newton Abbot, England

Cover design by Bill Paetzold
Cover illustration by Neal Hughes

First Printing, 1987
Printed in the United States of America
98 97 96 95 94 11 10 9 8 7

Library of Congress Cataloging-in-Publication Data
Levene, Nancy S., 1949-
French fry forgiveness
Summary: Alex joins the local swim team and quickly becomes enemies with another swimmer named Alexandria.
[1. Interpersonal relations—Fiction. 2. Swimming—Fiction.] I. Dorenkamp, Michelle, ill. II. TItle.
PZ7.L5724Fr 1987
[Fic] 87-5268
ISBN 1-55513-302-9

To my Heavenly Father
whose perfect time and perfect love
unceasingly increase my faith
and
To my parents,
Chuck and Jane Simpson,
in whom I see His gift to me.

But I say: Love your enemies! Pray for those who persecute you!
Matthew 5:44
The Living Bible

Your heavenly Father will forgive you if you forgive those who sin against you; but if you refuse to forgive them, he will not forgive you.
Matthew 6:14, 15
The Living Bible

ACKNOWLEDGMENTS

I praise God for Jeanne Rotert, who never failed in her encouragement and prayers for *ALEX*

and for

Ed Marquette, who shared his abundant suggestions, critiques, and Godly patience

and for

Ann and Lindsay, who laughed me out of the dark times.

Thank you, Karen and Vicky, for all your hard work.

CONTENTS

CHAPTER 1

An Enemy Strikes

"Aw, Mom, I'm already a good swimmer!" cried Alex. She folded her towel and placed it on her lap. *Why doesn't this car go faster? We'll never get there,* worried Alex. *And why does Mom keep talking about swimming lessons?*

"Okay, Alex," Mother sighed. "I just thought that you might need a little more help with your strokes . . . just to get them perfect," she quickly added noting the disgusted look on Alex's face. "There's a swimming class for your age group right after swim team practice. That would be perfect because it's the same time as your brother's swimming lesson."

"Brussels sprouts! I know that," Alex answered. "You've told me at least a hundred million times!''

''Hardly a million,'' commented her mother. ''Maybe only a hundred!'' She grinned at Alex.

''Blam! Pow! Gotcha!'' shrieked a voice behind Alex. She turned around and looked in the backseat. Two sparkling eyes and a wad of blond hair peeped out from under a beach towel.

''Whatcha shooting, Goblin?'' Alex asked her brother.

''Aliens!'' came his muffled reply.

''Oh, brother.'' Alex rolled her eyes at her mother. Mother just shrugged her shoulders as if to say, ''That's Rudy.''

Five-year-old Rudy's real name was David, but he had always called himself Rudy. Everyone in the family called him Rudy. Except Alex. She usually called him Goblin.

''Well, here we are,'' Mother announced as they turned onto the long driveway leading to the parking lot at the Kingswood Community Pool.

Alex jerked herself out of her memories. Why was she wasting time thinking about Rudy on the first day of swim team practice?

Mother parked the car in the first available

parking spot. Alex leaped out the door.

"Alex!" her mother exclaimed. "Get your towel! Do you have your sandals on? Slow down and wait for us!"

"Brussels sprouts!" muttered Alex. She grabbed her towel and forced herself to wait for her mother and Rudy. She could just glimpse part of the outside swimming pool.

"Rudy!" she heard Mother yell. "Get out of there this instant!"

"What's taking so long?" complained Alex. She hopped around the car to stand beside her mother. Mother was bent over, leaning into the car, grasping Rudy's legs with both hands. In fact, that was all Alex could see of her brother. The rest of him was under the front seat of the car.

"Goblin!" Alex exclaimed. She stamped both feet. He better not make her late!

Her brother, with help from Mother, wriggled out from under the seat and stumbled outside.

"Goblin, what's the big idea?" Alex demanded.

"Hiding," gulped Rudy breathlessly. "Aliens!" he whispered.

"Mom, I think he's seeing too many space movies," observed Alex.

Mother did not answer Alex. She just stood still and repeated over and over, "The Lord is my shepherd, the Lord is my shepherd. . . ."

This was a new practice in Alex's family. They had all decided that whenever one member of the family was angry with another member of the family, he or she would say, "The Lord is my shepherd" ten times before saying another word.

Her mother finished her verses and took a deep breath. "Okay," she said brightly, "let's go."

They began their walk to the swimming pool.

"Rudy, where is your towel?" asked Mother suddenly.

"Under the seat!" answered Rudy.

Mother got an I-am-going-to-explode-any-minute look on her face and stomped back to the car. Alex heard her saying, "The Lord is my shepherd, The Lord is my shepherd" from inside the car. She finally emerged from the car, holding Rudy's towel. "I can't believe it," was all she said to Alex.

"Come on, Goblin," Alex sighed.

As she got closer to the pool, Alex could see other children and one big man standing beside it. Alex began to feel just a little nervous. After all, she had never been on a swimming team before, and she didn't know anyone there.

The big man turned to meet them. "Hello," he said to Mother, "you must be Mrs. Brackenbury."

"That's right," answered Mother, "and this is my daughter, Alexandria. We call her Alex. She'd like to be on your team."

"Great! We will be happy to have her on the team," the man responded. "Alex, I'm the coach. My name is Bob. You can call me Coach or Bob or Coach Bob. How old are you, Alex?"

"Eight," replied Alex.

"Your mom tells me you're a top-rate softball player," winked Coach Bob. "Is that true?"

Alex grinned. "I'm the pitcher for the Tornadoes," she said proudly.

"Well, I'm glad to have an athlete like you on our team. We're called the Sharks." He looked around. "Guess we better get practice started. We always warm up with a few exercises. Mrs.

Brackenbury, you can sit over there.'' The coach pointed to some chairs where other mothers were seated. Alex watched her mother and Rudy walk away. Rudy's head was completely covered with his towel.

''By the way, Alex,'' said Coach Bob, ''we have another Alexandria here . . . although I don't think she'd want us to call her Alex.'' He gave a low chuckle.

A tall, slim girl in a lavender bathing suit gave her long, blonde hair a flip. ''No way!'' she answered loudly. ''And,'' she added looking straight at Alex, ''I think softball is boring!''

Halfway through swim practice, Alex was exhausted. She had done fifteen minutes of warm-up exercises and had swum what seemed like thousands of short sprints across the pool and back. She felt weak and quivery. Softball practice wasn't this hard! She glanced at the big, round clock above the concession stand. Still forty-five minutes to go. Alex wondered if she could make it. Half floating at the side of the pool while resting her aching arms on the concrete,

she tried to catch her breath.

"What's the matter, *A-A-A-Alex*?" shouted a sarcastic voice behind her. "Whoever heard of a girl called *Alex*?"

Alex whirled her head around. A face with blonde hair floating around it was sneering at her. Alex knew that face. Alexandria!

"The hotshot ballplayer can't take it," giggled another blonde-haired girl. They both swam around Alex and quickly sprung out of the pool.

Alex's face turned red. She heaved herself out of the water. She was not going to be made fun of by those two!

"Okay, everybody out of the pool," shouted Coach Bob. "Let's go down to the deep end. We'll do some long-distance swimming."

Several groans were heard. Long-distance swimming? Alex slowly followed the group toward the deep end. Suddenly a hand gripped her shoulder. Alex jumped! Then she relaxed. It was the coach. "How ya doing, Alex?"

"Okay, I guess," mumbled Alex.

"Don't worry, you'll get used to these workouts," he assured her. "These kids have all been practicing through the winter. You'll catch up with them."

Alex gave him a sickly smile. Her legs were shaking, and she'd swallowed so much water that it seemed as if half the swimming pool was inside of her. She trudged on.

Coach Bob hurried ahead to the other swimmers. "Line up!" he called. "I want the ten-year-old-and-under swimmers in the outside lanes. Swim to the shallow end, get out, walk—and I mean walk—back to this end and swim it again. The older ones take the middle lanes.

Swim down the right side of the lanes and back up the left side of the lanes. Thirty laps! Okay! Let's Go!"

Shreeeee! Coach Bob's whistle pierced the air. He blew a blast each time a swimmer was to start.

Alex tiredly took a place at the end of one of the lines on the right side of the pool. She gazed at the shallow end. It seemed pretty far! How many times were they going to do this?

Shreeee! Shreeee! Shreeee! The kids in front of her were rapidly disappearing into the water. Soon it was Alex's turn. She moved up to the edge of the pool and got ready to dive.

"Oh, dear, excuuuuse me!" a loud voice cried. Alex felt someone push her from behind. She tried, tottering and waving her arms, to keep her balance, but her foot slipped and Alex found herself falling. She had no doubt who had pushed her. Even as she fell and splashed loudly into the water, her mind screamed, *ALEXANDRIA!*

CHAPTER 2

Last in the Race

Alex came up out of the water choking and sputtering. She had just been pushed off the edge of the swimming pool! Loud laughter greeted her. It sounded as if the whole swimming team was laughing at her. Shading her eyes from the sun, Alex squinted at the swimmers above her. She didn't see Alexandria, but she was sure that Alexandria had pushed her.

Shreeee! Shreeee! Shreeee! Coach Bob's whistle was still blowing and swimmers were diving over her head! Didn't Coach Bob see what happened to her? Didn't he care?

All at once the whistle stopped shrieking. "Who's in the water?" demanded the coach. "Alex?"

Alex turned around in the water and looked at

him. She wanted to tell him what happened.

"Alex! That's not a very safe place to rest," called her coach. "If you're tired, go sit on the concrete."

Alex climbed out of the pool and got back in line. She would show Coach Bob that she wasn't tired. She would show everyone that she could swim just as far as they could. A few kids looked at her and giggled. Alex bit her lip and ignored them.

Shreeee! Alex dove into the water. She kicked and thrashed her way to the end of the pool. She was so upset that tears ran out of her eyes and mixed with the pool water. *Quit crying,* she told herself. *Everyone will think you're a baby!*

Time after time after time Alex swam the length of the pool, climbed out, walked back to the other end, and swam it again. She stayed as far away from Alexandria as she could and kept a sharp lookout behind her each time she got ready to dive.

Finally, just as Alex thought she could not make it one more time, the whistle stopped blowing.

''Sharks!'' Coach Bob yelled. ''I want to record swimming times for all of you. Divide up into your groups. The first four groups will swim two lengths of the pool. The last four groups will swim one length. I'll call out your time when you're finished. Remember it! That's the time you'll be trying to improve for our first summer swim meet.''

Everyone scrambled, pushing and shoving, to find their groups. Alex felt completely lost. She made her way over to where the coach was standing. He was staring at a stopwatch. Alex tapped his arm.

''Oh, Alex,'' he said, ''I'm sorry. I forgot about you. You'll be in the last group, okay? You can sit and rest until I call your group.''

Before Alex could ask him any questions, he began shouting to the first group of swimmers, ''Five seconds to go!''

Alex looked the first group over carefully. The oldest swimmers were lined up across the pool at the shallow end. They all stood on starting blocks.

The swimmers bent into diving positions.

Shreeee! went the whistle. They dove with long, shallow dives that took them far out into the pool. With smooth, powerful strokes, they rapidly skimmed the surface of the water, their kicking feet barely making a splash. Alex could hardly tell when a swimmer took a breath! *If only I could swim like that,* Alex wished.

In no time at all, the swimmers reached the deep end. To Alex's joy, they gracefully flipped underwater and came back up again swimming in the other direction.

The race was ending. The coach called out different numbers to each swimmer as he or she reached the shallow end.

"Fifty-one! Sixty-one! Sixty-two! . . ."

With close attention, Alex watched the next race and the next race and the next race. She was determined that someday soon she would swim like these swimmers!

At the beginning of the fifth race, Alexandria stood on a block. Alex stared at Alexandria's long, blonde hair tied back behind her head and her lavender swimming suit with tiny white stripes running through it. All at once, Alex became aware of her own short, brown hair and plain blue swimming suit.

Alexandria's group swam only one length of the pool. Alexandria came in first. Alex listened for her time.

"Thirty-six," Coach Bob shouted. *That must be a good time since she won her race,* thought Alex. *I wonder what my time will be?* She waited nervously for the last group to be called.

After two more races, Coach Bob shouted "Last group!" Alex got up off the concrete. She looked around her as she walked to the shallow end. Only the smallest children were left. "Brussels sprouts! I must be racing with the six-year-olds!" muttered Alex. To make matters worse, Alexandria was watching Alex with a smug grin on her face. *She's gonna make fun of me,* worried Alex.

Alex stepped up onto one of the starting blocks. She felt awfully high up in the air. *What if I crash into the bottom of the pool when I dive off this thing? After all, it is the shallow end.*

As if he could hear her thoughts, Coach Bob jogged around to where she was. "Now, Alex," he said, "you don't have to dive off the blocks if you don't want to at first. You can dive off the edge of the pool. Have you ever done this before?"

Alex shook her head.

"Well, you have to dive far out and flat. Don't dive deep!" He looked at her for a moment. "Do you want to try it?"

Alex was aware of everyone staring at her, especially Alexandria. She couldn't chicken out now! "Sure, I can do it!" Alex told the coach. She sounded a lot braver than she felt.

Coach Bob trotted back to the deep end. "Five seconds!" he yelled.

Alex, imitating the others, moved up to the edge of the starting block and curled her toes around it. She bent into the diving position.

Shreeee!

Alex stopped breathing. She dove out as far as she could and as flat as she could. Plop, splash! Alex landed flat on her stomach.

Ouch! Kick, splash, breathe, splash, kick. . . . Alex beat the water as she swam as fast as she could. She finally touched the edge at the deep end of the pool.

"Fifty!" Coach Bob yelled in her ear.

"Brussels sprouts! That's way more than Alexandria," Alex told herself. She looked around. Nobody else was in the pool. Everyone was gathering up their towels and walking away. "I must have been the last one in my group. Even the little kids beat me!" Alex felt embarrassed and discouraged.

She hung onto the side of the pool, letting her legs float in the water. She didn't feel like getting out. She didn't feel like doing anything.

"Gotcha! Pow!" A stream of cold water hit Alex's face. She shook the water out of her eyes and looked up. Rudy stood above her, grinning and pointing his squirt gun at her.

All the anger Alex had felt this morning exploded inside of her. She half leaped out of the pool, grabbed Rudy's legs and flung him into the water.

"Goblin!" she yelled in his ear. She dunked him underwater. "Don't try that again!" She dunked him a second time. "And leave me alone!" She dunked him again.

Rudy came up hollering, choking, and wildly thrashing in the deep water.

“Alex! Stop that!” Mother appeared at the pool’s edge.

Alex let go of Rudy. He sank underwater.

“Alex! Grab him!” shouted Mother.

Alex grabbed her brother and pushed him to the edge. Rudy quickly scrambled up beside Mother. “My squirt gun’s lost!” he howled.

“Good!” responded Alex.

“Alex, it’s dangerous to dunk Rudy in the deep water,” her mother told her. “You know he can’t swim very well.''

''I can, too!'' Rudy shouted.

Mother gave him a long look. He closed his mouth.

''Alex I believe you forgot to say 'The Lord is my shepherd' ten times before you threw your brother in the water,'' reminded her mother.

Alex thought about that for a moment. ''But Mom, what if I say 'The Lord is my shepherd', ten times and still want to throw him in the water?'' she asked.

Mother smiled. ''Then say it ten more times, honey,'' she answered.

''But, what if I still want to . . .'' Alex began.

''Say it another ten times.''

''Brussels sprouts! With Rudy around I could be saying 'The Lord is my shepherd' my whole life!'' Alex exclaimed.

''Hmmmm,'' reflected Mother, ''that's not such a bad idea, Alex.''

She turned to Rudy. ''As for you, young man, we will have a special rule for you! Whenever you are tempted to do something *wrong* to someone else, you should say 'The Lord is my shepherd' ten times."

Alex shook her head. "It won't work, Mom!"

"Oh, you might be surprised, Alex," said her mother, "the Lord's power is very strong."

They both looked at Rudy. *The Lord would have to use His superduper power on Rudy—like when He opened the sea for Moses,* thought Alex.

Rudy squirmed uncomfortably under their gaze. "I want my squirt gun!" he whined.

Mother sighed. "Come on, Rudy, your swimming lesson is starting. Alex, we'll be over at the lap pool. Please, find his gun for him."

"Aw, Mom," complained Alex.

Her mother gave her one of those don't-cause-me-anymore-trouble looks and led Rudy off to his class.

Alex began diving for the gun. She found it on her third dive and threw it over the edge of the pool. She slowly climbed out of the water and walked over to her towel. It was the only one left lying on the cement. It looked lonely. That was how Alex felt—lonely—the only one left—the last one.

She walked down to the shallow end. The starting blocks were still there. Alex crawled up on one of the blocks and sat there for a while gazing out at the water. "Maybe I oughta just stick with softball," she sighed. She wiggled to the edge of the block and let her feet dangle in the water.

The first day of swim practice and everything went wrong, she thought, angrily kicking the water. *I have an enemy on the team and I can't dive without killing my stomach and I'm the slowest swimmer on the team!* She gave the water an extrahard kick! SPLASH!

"Hey!" a voice cried behind her. "You're getting me all wet!"

Alex whirled around. Coach Bob was standing there smiling at her.

"Alex, you look rather sad sitting out here all by yourself," he told her. "You know, the first day of practice is always the hardest."

"Yeah, but I was rotten!" exclaimed Alex. "Even the littlest kids beat me!"

"Not for long," declared Coach Bob. "I think that after a few more weeks of practice, you'll be right up there competing with the best of them."

"A few more weeks," groaned Alex. "That's a long time."

"Not really," he replied. "To do anything well takes practice. You didn't learn how to pitch in one day, did you?"

"No way!" Alex exclaimed.

"Well, it's the same way with swimming. Now come on, I'll help you with your strokes and your diving."

"Right now?" Alex asked hopefully.

"Right now!"

CHAPTER 3

Battle Begins

"Oh, come on, Mom, say 'yes.' All the kids are counting on you!"

"Barbara—" began Mother.

"You already said you weren't busy this Saturday . . . please!"

"I've told you before, Barbara. I'll have to talk to your father first."

Alex sighed. Even though she was sitting on the front steps outside her house, she still could hear her older sister begging Mom to let her have a party. "Miss Mushy's been yacking about a party all afternoon," Alex complained to herself. How boring! Alex believed that most of what her older sister did was boring.

Blam! Alex heard the back door slam. "Miss Mushy must have given up for a while," she decided. "She's probably going out now to sunbathe some more." Alex shook her head. "Brussels sprouts! Who would wanna lie in the sun doin' nothing? I hope when I get to be almost thirteen like Miss Mushy I don't do dumb things like that."

Recently, Alex had begun to wonder what it would be like to be thirteen. It seemed awfully old and, well, kind of scary. She made a disgusted face and bounced her softball down the steps. *Still,* she thought, *Miss Mushy's always talking about how neat it will be to be a teenager, so maybe it isn't so bad.* "Oh, well, I'm glad I'm only eight," she sighed.

"Alex! Hey, Alex! You wanna see my turtles?"

Alex looked up.

Jason, her next door neighbor, was slowly moving down the sidewalk on his hands and knees.

Alex left her softball at the bottom of the steps and walked over to Jason. Two middle-sized box turtles inched their way along the sidewalk, one after the other.

"See, Alex, isn't he neat?" cried Jason excitedly. He grabbed up one of the turtles and held it up for Alex to see. "I found him in the creek!"

"Yeah, I guess so," Alex replied. *Why does this kid like turtles so much,* she wondered. "What does Clementine think of him?" asked Alex, pointing to the other turtle. "Isn't she jealous?"

"Of course not!" Jason sounded surprised. "This is a boy turtle. Clementine's a girl turtle. They're gonna get married and have lots of babies!"

"Oh, good grief!" sighed Alex.

"Eeeeyaaaaoooooo—pow!" Two feet leaped over the sidewalk, barely missing the turtles.

"Watch it, Rudy!" shrieked Jason. "You might hurt 'em!"

Rudy turned a couple of flips in the yard. "Whatacha doin', Jason?" he asked.

"Just taking Clementine and Homer for a walk."

"Clementine and who?" Rudy asked.

"Homer," repeated Alex to her brother. She suddenly noticed that he had her softball in his hand. "Gimme that ball!"

"Come and get it," laughed Rudy, jumping backwards.

Alex lunged for the ball. Before she could reach it, Rudy threw the ball up over his head backwards as hard as he could. The ball sailed behind him several feet into the street.

Thud, SMACK! It hit the side of a passing car. SCREECH! The car swerved a bit, then zoomed into their driveway. It was their father's car!

"Brussels sprouts! You hit Dad's car!" Alex shouted at Rudy.

"Alex! Rudy! Get over here!" bellowed their father.

"You've had it now, Goblin," warned Alex.

"What's going on here?" asked Father as Alex hurried up to him. Rudy followed at a much slower pace. "Who threw that ball?" demanded Father. "I thought it was going to hit my windshield!" Father checked the side of the car but could find no marks. Alex told her father what had happened.

"Rudy, go to your room until dinner," ordered Father. "Hitting cars with balls is dangerous business. It could cause an accident."

"But I didn't mean to!" Rudy howled.

"That doesn't matter! It still happened," stated his father. "Now go to your room!

"Better try and find your ball, Firecracker," Father told Alex. "Firecracker" was Father's special name for Alex.

"Well, well, what's this? A parade?" boomed Father. Jason and the turtles had made their way slowly up to the driveway.

"Oh, that's Clementine, Homer, and Jason," Alex said.

"I do believe I know Jason," Father chuckled, "and I already have had the honor of meeting Clementine, my darling." Father made a low bow. "But as for Homer, I have not had the pleasure."

Alex giggled at her father bowing to a turtle. Then she told him, "Jason found Homer in the creek. Don't you think they make a nice couple?"

"Who, Jason and Homer?" asked her father with a wink.

"No!" laughed Alex. "Clementine and

Homer. Jason says they're gonna get married."

"Aha, hmmmm." Father stroked his chin and looked at the turtles. "A splendid couple, no doubt about it." He clapped Jason on the shoulders, then turned to Alex. "Better get your ball, Firecracker, and come inside. I'm sure it's almost time for dinner."

"Good, Alex! Forty-six seconds! That's four seconds off your time from yesterday," Coach Bob yelled in her ear.

Alex climbed out of the pool. She felt better

about swimming today. The other swimmers were still coming in ahead of her, but she was getting faster. She had tried hard to swim her strokes the way her coach had shown her yesterday.

"You're still slapping the water," Coach Bob told her. "Make your strokes smooth but powerful." He moved his arms to demonstrate. "Pull underwater!"

"Okay," gasped Alex. She got out and walked around the side of the pool. As she passed Alexandria and a group of her friends, giggles and snickers burned her ears. Someone shouted, "SLAP! SLAP! SLAP!" followed by more giggles and snickers.

Alex sat down on the concrete several feet away from the group. Her face was red and she felt hot and shaky. *Brussels sprouts! Why don't they leave me alone? I haven't done anything to them!*

"Okay, everybody, pick up a board and into the water!" hollered Coach Bob.

Alex, still upset, waited for everyone else to grab a kickboard and jump into the pool before she got in.

"First four groups—forty laps across the pool! Second four groups—twenty! Ready? Go!" their coach shouted.

Groans were heard, but the swimmers began kicking. Alex and several others were soon left behind. Kicking feet ahead of her splashed water into her face.

Twenty laps! Can I do it? Across and back, across and back. Her muscles were sore. Her entire body ached.

"Feet together! Toes pointed!" Coach Bob yelled.

Four, three, two, one more lap to go, Alex counted. She half floated the last lap and finally reached the edge.

"That's it for today," she heard Coach Bob announce. Suddenly something hit Alex's face! It knocked her off balance. She slipped underwater. When she came up she saw her towel floating in the water beside her. She also saw Coach Bob coming toward her, dragging Alexandria by the arm!

"I saw you throw that towel!" he yelled at

Alexandria. ''What's the big idea? You owe Alex an apology and a dry towel!''

Alex got out of the pool.

''Well?'' growled Coach Bob, looking angrily at Alexandria.

''Sorry,'' said Alexandria in a way that let Alex know she wasn't sorry at all.

Alex just stared at her. She was no longer sad. She was mad!

Coach Bob looked disgusted. He grabbed Alexandria's towel and held it out to Alex. ''Here, Alex, you can dry off with this towel.''

Alex snatched the towel from his hand. Looking straight at Alexandria, she hissed, ''I wouldn't use this towel for a million bucks.'' Very calmly, Alex dropped Alexandria's towel into the water and walked away.

For Alex, the war had begun!

CHAPTER 4

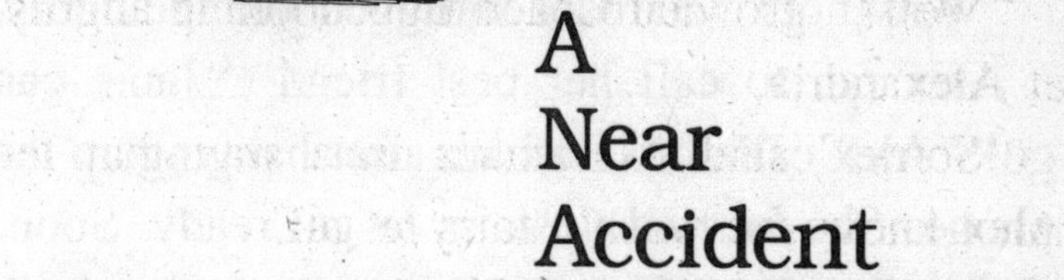

A Near Accident

“I’m sorry Alex, but I can’t take you to the pool this afternoon,” said Mother.

“I could ride my bike,” Alex pleaded.

“No, not by yourself,” Mother answered.

“Mom, I need to get in some extra practice for swim team,” cried Alex.

“I’m sorry, Alex.”

“I’ll go with her,” Barbara offered suddenly.

Alex and Mother stared at her.

“I could work on my tan,” Barbara said in answer to their surprised looks.

Miss Mushy is being awfully nice this week, thought Alex. *She’s probably trying to show Mom that she deserves a party.*

“Well, I guess that would be okay,” agreed

Mother a little suspiciously.

"Whoopee!" shouted Alex. "Can Janie come, too?" she asked her sister.

"Why not?" Barbara shrugged her shoulders.

Alex ran to call her best friend. "Janie can go!" Alex called to Barbara after hanging up the phone. She hurried upstairs to get ready. Soon, CLUMP, CLUMP, CLUMP, she was back downstairs, dressed in her bathing suit and lugging a filled-to-the-top beach bag. Alex groaned as she swung it over her shoulder.

"What do you have in there?" asked Barbara.

"Just things I need—like goggles, flippers, a few toys, money, oh, and my tire."

"Your tire!" Barbara exclaimed.

"Yeah! Don't worry. I'll wait and blow it up at the pool," replied Alex.

"Oh, boy," sighed Barbara. "Can you carry all that stuff on your bike?"

"Sure! Oh, wait, I forgot my beach ball." CLUMP, CLUMP, CLUMP! Alex quickly ran upstairs and back down again. She clutched a giant blue ball in her hands. "Janie's here!" she yelled excitedly, looking out the front door.

"I don't know if I'm ready for all of this," mumbled Barbara.

"We're ready to go!" Alex hollered at her mother.

Mother walked out of the kitchen. "Okay, girls, now be careful and stay right with Barbara. Watch the traffic. Barbara, you lead the way and stick close together."

"Don't worry, Mom. What can happen in a few blocks?"

"Plenty!" answered Mother. She looked Alex over. "How are you going to ride with all those things in your hands?"

"Easy! I'll put the bag over my shoulder and put the ball in my basket."

"Will it stay in your basket?" asked Mother.

"Sure!"

"Do you have a towel, Alex?"

Alex threw everything on the floor and ran back upstairs. CLUMP! CLUMP! CLUMP! CLUMP! She and her towel jumped down the last five steps.

"Come on, before I change my mind," warned Barbara.

The three girls dashed out to their bikes.

"Be careful and have fun!" called Mother from the doorway.

Alex quickly tied her towel around her waist, threw her beach bag over her shoulder, and stuffed the ball in her basket. It didn't exactly fit. It kept popping out of the basket. "Oh, well, I can hold it in there and ride with one hand," she told herself. "It's not too far to the pool."

"Let's go!" cried Barbara.

Janie and Alex grinned at each other and followed Barbara out of the driveway and down the street.

"Faster!" called Alex.

"This is fast enough!" shouted Barbara over her shoulder. "Single file! Alex, get in back of Janie! We're coming to the first traffic light." They stopped at the corner.

When the light turned green, Barbara started across the street, followed by Janie, followed by—Alex's bike suddenly stopped. She was halfway across the street and her pedals wouldn't turn! She looked down. Her towel had slipped from around her waist and was wrapped around

one of the pedals! She yanked on it. It wouldn't come loose!

"Help!" she screeched. The light was turning yellow. In a few seconds, all those cars would start up and run right over her!

Barbara, on the other side of the street was wildly waving her arms and yelling, "Get out of the street!"

Alex did the only thing she could think of. She dropped the bike right there in the middle of the street and ran as fast as she could to the other side.

Barbara grabbed Alex and held onto her as if she thought Alex would suddenly dart back into the street. Janie stood on the sidewalk with her hands over her eyes.

The light changed. They all held their breath, waiting for the cars to smash Alex's bicycle to pieces.

Seconds passed. Nobody moved—not Alex, not Barbara, not Janie, and not any of the cars. Alex could hardly stand it. "Somebody do something," she screamed to herself.

Somebody did. A man jumped out of the first

car in line. He trotted over to the bike, picked it up, and hurriedly carried it over to the girls.

Cars on both sides of the street began honking and people began cheering. The man raced back to his car. Traffic began moving normally. People in the cars smiled and pointed at the three girls. Janie finally uncovered her eyes.

"Alex!" Barbara exclaimed. "What in the world happened?"

Before Alex could explain, a policeman on a motorcycle pulled up beside them. "What's the trouble, girls?" he asked.

Alex could only stare at him. A policeman? Brussels sprouts! Janie covered her eyes again.

"Uh," Barbara stammered, "my sister, uh, somehow fell off her bike in the middle of the street."

"Uh-huh," he answered slowly looking at Alex. "You caused quite a traffic jam."

"I'm sorry," Alex answered. "I didn't mean to and I didn't fall off my bike. I jumped off! My towel got stuck in the pedal."

"Hmmm," replied the policeman.

"Are you gonna give us a ticket?" Alex asked,

feeling a little braver. Barbara gasped.

"Well . . . I don't think so," answered the policeman. He was smiling now. "But make sure that doesn't happen again. You could have been hurt badly. When you carry things on your bicycle you must be certain that they can't come loose or fall off and cause an accident."

"Yes, sir," said Alex. Out of the corner of her eye she noticed that her beach ball wasn't in her bicycle basket anymore. Where was it?

The police officer told them to be careful and drove away.

"Whew!" sighed Barbara. "Let's get to the pool. You can uncover your eyes now, Janie. Alex, why'd you ask him if he was going to give us a ticket?"

Alex shrugged. "I just wondered if he would. Where's my ball?"

"Your what?" asked Barbara.

"My beach ball! It was in my basket, and now it's not there anymore!"

"I have no idea," answered Barbara, exasperated. "Don't worry about a ball. You're lucky to have your bike in one piece. Help me get this towel off the pedal!''

''I see the ball!'' cried Janie. She pointed. Alex looked. It was under a bush by the sidewalk. She ran to get it. Barbara yanked the towel loose. Only a couple of grease spots showed on it.

''I'll carry the towel and the ball,'' Barbara told Alex. ''You put your beach bag in your basket.''

''Alex, are you going to tell your mother about this?'' Janie asked.

Alex and Janie stared at one another. Alex knew that Janie was remembering a time last spring when Alex had told her mother several lies. She had gotten in a huge mess because of them.

''Yeah, I better tell her,'' answered Alex.

''Come on. Let's go,'' ordered Barbara.

The girls got on their bikes and once more headed for the swimming pool. They arrived with no further trouble. Alex and Janie immediately blew up Alex's tire and floated around the pool, jumping in and out of it and swimming underneath it.

Barbara ''worked'' on her tan with several

other girls her age. Alex wondered how anyone could call it "work." All they did was lie on chairs or towels in the sun and talk. Once in a while they would jump in the water to cool off.

Alex and Janie had just come back to their towels from a third trip to the snack bar. They flopped down to eat already melting ice-cream sandwiches and sip on grape-flavored snow cones. Barbara walked over to them. "We need to get going soon, Alex."

"Aw no," complained Alex and Janie together.

"It's five o'clock, and Mom wants us home by five thirty," Barbara told Alex.

"Oh, okay, just let us finish eating this stuff," Alex replied.

"Well, don't take too long."

As soon as she left, Alex grabbed Janie's arm. "Look," she whispered. "There's Alexandria! See? Over there. That's the mean girl I was telling you about!"

"Where? Where? Oh, yeah," Janie whispered back. "Did she really throw your towel in the water?"

"Yeah," Alex exclaimed, "and she pushed me in the water the first day of practice!"

"Boy, what a creep!" exploded Janie. They continued to stare at Alexandria.

"I thought someone that mean would be ugly," Janie finally remarked.

Alex thought that over and said slowly, "You know, Janie, she is ugly! She's ugly inside herself."

"Yeah, my mom always says that it's what's inside your heart that counts," said Janie.

"Right!" agreed Alex. "Alexandria must have a real, ugly heart!"

CHAPTER 5

The Fight

On the third day of swim team practice, Alex felt a lot better. She wasn't falling quite so far behind the others. While swimming the short sprints across the pool she actually managed to beat some of the younger swimmers! She looked forward to swimming the length of the pool with her group. She was sure her time would be much faster.

After swimming her laps with a kickboard, Alex climbed out of the pool to get her goggles. She hadn't needed them just to kick and had laid them on top of her towel at the side of the pool. Where were they? Here was her towel, but the goggles were nowhere to be seen. Alex shook her towel out again. Nothing fell from it.

"Are you looking for your goggles?" a voice

asked her. Alex looked up. Standing beside her was a girl about her age named Shellie.

Alex answered, "Yeah, I guess I lost them."

"You didn't lose them," replied Shellie. "Look!"

Alex's eyes followed Shellie's pointed finger. There, hanging on the very top part of the fence, were Alex's goggles.

"How'd they get there?" wondered Alex.

"Guess," Shellie answered.

"Alexandria!" exclaimed Alex. Shellie nodded.

"Thanks," mumbled Alex. She ran over to the fence and stood looking up at her goggles. "Brussels sprouts, I'll have to climb the fence to reach them," she exclaimed to herself.

Climbing fences was no hard job for Alex. It just made her angry to have to do it. "Alexandria has no right to touch my stuff," she muttered to herself. "She's always starting trouble! If she wants trouble, I'll give her trouble! She'll see I can be just as mean as she is!"

By the time Alex climbed down from the fence, she was fuming. She turned toward the pool.

There, standing near the edge of the pool, were Alexandria and her friends. They were watching Alex and laughing hilariously. That was too much for Alex. Something snapped inside of her. She charged full speed across the concrete into the middle of the group. She would have attacked them all if she could, but her main target was Alexandria.

Alex hit Alexandria and two others so hard that all four of them plummeted into the water! Alex landed right on top of Alexandria. She grabbed a handful of blonde hair and pulled—hard! She kicked her feet against Alexandria's back. She screamed in her ears. No other swimmer dared to go near them.

Strong arms grabbed Alex from behind. "ALEX! LET GO!" "ALEX! LET GO!"

Alex finally let loose of Alexandria's hair. She collapsed in the arms that held her. She knew they were the coach's arms. Sobs shook her body.

Alex felt Coach Bob pull her through the water. He had a hold of Alexandria with his other arm. He boosted Alexandria up over the edge, then climbed out of the pool still carrying Alex under his arm. Alex felt like a little kid, but she didn't care. She didn't think she could walk anyway. Her legs felt like rubber.

The coach set her down on the concrete and made Alexandria sit down, too. He instructed the other swimmers to swim some laps. Then he sat down between the two girls.

"What's going on here?" he asked. "Nothing like this has ever happened before on my swim team in all the years I've been coaching! Would one of you please explain?"

Coach Bob looked first at Alexandria. She only stared at the other swimmers in the pool and wouldn't look at him.

He turned his head and looked at Alex. Alex looked up at him. She felt terrible. She wanted to tell him everything, but she could not be a tattle-tale. Besides, she didn't understand it either. Tears came to her eyes and she quickly ducked her head.

"All right!" Coach Bob threw up his hands. "You don't have to tell me anything, but I want this kind of behavior to stop. There is no room for fighting on my team. You two girls are finished for today. You may go home.''

Alexandria quickly picked up her towel and stalked away.

Alex went to find her mother and Rudy. She found them sitting at a table on a balcony overlooking the pool. Rudy was sipping on an orange drink, dangerously tipping his chair backwards. ''Rudy! Sit on the chair right!'' Alex heard her mother say as she made her way over to them. She dropped into a chair beside Rudy.

''Alex!'' Mother exclaimed. ''What in the world happened down there? One minute I saw you swimming, and the next minute I saw you knocking kids into the water and fighting with some girl in the pool.''

Alex put her elbows on the table and leaned her head in her hands. ''That girl is Alexandria, Mom, and yesterday she threw my towel in the water and the day before she pushed me into the water and today she took my goggles and hung them on the fence and I had to climb up and get them and all her friends were laughing at me! I got really mad and just had to start fighting her back. I just had to.''

''Whoa! Slow down, Alex. Maybe you better start at the beginning. I'm not understanding this too well,'' replied Mother. ''Rudy! You'll fall over backwards if you keep tilting your chair like that.''

Alex took a deep breath and, beginning with the first day of swim practice, told her mother all that had happened between her and Alexandria. When she had finished she felt relieved. It was good to share her problems with someone else instead of keeping them all inside herself. Why didn't she remember that whenever she got in trouble?

''Well! This is a tough one, Alex,'' her mother said gently. ''I can certainly understand why you felt angry and why you lost your temper. But Alex, honey, do you think that what you did today was the right thing to do?''

''Ummm, before now, I thought that I would feel better if I could hurt Alexandria the way she hurt me,'' Alex said slowly.

''And do you feel better now?'' her mother asked.

“Not really.” Alex’s head and hands sank lower on the table. She tried not to look down at the pool below her. Practice was still going on. The swimmers were racing in their groups with Coach Bob checking their times.

“Mom, it’s so unfair!” Alex blurted.

“There are a lot of things that are unfair in this world, Alex. Someday we will live in a perfect world with Jesus, but we aren’t there yet.”

“Yeah, but what am I supposed to do right now, Mom? I can’t wait a hundred more years till I go to Heaven to figure out what to do about Alexandria!”

Mother laughed, “I don’t think you’ll have to wait that long, Alex.” She reached for Alex’s hands and held them. She asked quietly, “Have you given this problem to the Lord, Alex?”

“Huh? What do you mean?” Alex questioned. “How can I give it to the Lord?”

“By asking Him to take it,” Mother explained. “Instead of you trying to deal with Alexandria yourself, ask the Lord to handle the whole thing. He will show you how to solve your problem.”

“There’s one more thing, Alex,” added Moth-

er. ‘‘You can’t carry hatred around in your heart against Alexandria. The Bible says we have to forgive our enemies and do good to them.’’

‘‘Do good to Alexandria! Impossible!’’ cried Alex.

‘‘Nothing’s impossible with God,’’ Mother insisted.

At that instant there was a BANG! and a CRASH! Rudy’s chair and Rudy fell to the floor. For a moment complete silence filled the room. Alex knew that everyone was looking at them. He’s so embarrassing, she thought.

Rudy's mouth screwed up and let out a high-pitched scream. Alex thought that scream would never end. *Why does he just lie there and yell? If it was me, even if my head hurt, I'd jump up and pick up my chair and sit at the table real fast so everybody'd quit looking at me!*

"Alex, help me!" ordered Mother. She was trying to pull Rudy off the floor, but he refused to let go of the chair. Mother could not get both hands loose at the same time. He was still screaming.

"Alex, I need to take Rudy to the bathroom to clean him up. If you want to come sit with me while he has his swimming lesson, you can," offered Mother.

"Aw, no thanks," Alex answered. "I got some thinking to do." She watched her mother drag Rudy off to the bathroom. He was sniveling loudly. Orange drink dripped down his legs.

Alex left the table and ran down the balcony steps. She picked out a big, shady tree by the pool and sat down under it. It was still early enough in the morning that no one else was around. She could hear noise from Rudy's swimming group, but as they were using another pool it didn't bother her.

Alex didn't waste any time. She got on her knees and quietly whispered, "Dear Lord Jesus, please tell me what to do about Alexandria. I really need Your help. And . . . Lord, I'm sorry for the fighting today. Amen."

Alex sprawled under the tree. She felt better, but somehow she knew that something was missing.

Tiny ripples fluttered across the water in front of her. They made endless flowing lines across the pool. As Alex watched them, she remembered her talk with her mother a few minutes ago. Every word came back to her.

Oh! Alex sat straight up. *That's it! Brussels sprouts! Mom said I shouldn't hate Alexandria. I should do good to her and forgive her.* Her heart sank. *How can I ever do that? Alexandria doesn't deserve anything good. She's always trying to make me mad. She must hate me! Why should I do good to her? Why should I forgive her?*

Alex sat remembering all the hateful things Alexandria had done to her. There was no reason for her to have been so mean. *I never did anything to her.*

You did something bad to Alexandria today, she reminded herself. *But she started it! I couldn't help pushing her into the water. I was too mad!*

Alex stood up quickly. Too many confusing thoughts were battling in her head.

SPLASH! The ripples on the pool turned to waves as she dove into the water. Alex swam to the shallow end. She got up on a starting block and looked at the clock. She was going to see how long it took her to get to the deep end. She'd check her own time. She waited until the red second hand reached the twelve, then dove as far out and as shallow as she could.

Time after time after time Alex checked the clock and swam the length of the pool. She didn't notice her coach watching her. She didn't even notice Mother and Rudy watching and waiting for her. She swam to silence the battle. She swam to forget Alexandria. She swam and swam and swam.

CHAPTER 6

Miss Mushy

"Mom! Get him out of here. He's ruining everything!"

"Now, Barbara, take it easy," soothed Mother as she came to the back door from the kitchen, where she had been preparing all kinds of snacks for Barbara's party.

The big party was tonight, and everyone in the family was scurrying around getting ready for it. Everyone, that is, except Rudy. He was trying his best to get in the way.

Alex was perched on a limb of the big oak tree that stood at one corner of the patio. She had tied the end of a bright red streamer around the limb. Her sister, standing on the top rung of a ladder, had just about tied her end of the streamer to a corner of the house when Rudy leaped into the air and broke the streamer in two!

"See what he did!" Barbara wailed to her mother. "Now we have to start all over."

"Rudy! Come inside right now," Mother ordered.

Barbara handed the streamer roll back up to Alex. "Disgusting little brat," she muttered.

"Disgusting is right," Alex grumbled silently. Only she couldn't decide who was the more disgusting—Rudy or Barbara. "It's hard enough trying to hang up these goofy streamers, but Miss Mushy has to have them twisted in little tiny curliques!"

"Watch it, Alex! You're wrinkling the streamer!" cried Barbara.

"I'll wrinkle you in a minute," Alex muttered under her breath. Before hanging the streamers, they had had to wash the patio three times! Miss Mushy wanted it to sparkle. Before washing the patio, they had had to plant petunias all around the oak tree exactly nine inches apart! Miss Mushy wanted it pretty. Before planting the petunias, they had had to trim all the bushes! Miss Mushy wanted it neat.

"Pppt! Tunia!" growled Alex.

"What did you say?" Barbara called to Alex.

"Nothing." Alex wondered what her next assignment would be.

"Got it!" her sister exclaimed. "Now, I'm going to tie another one from here over to that smaller tree."

"Terrific," Alex mumbled. She curled both legs around the limb of the tree, leaned back, and let her head and arms drop down. She was getting ready to skin-the-cat—the only respectable way to get down from a tree.

"Wait!" Barbara hollered. "Don't get down yet. I need you to hang a lantern up there. I'll go get it."

"Brussels sprouts!" Alex hung by her knees and waited for her sister. A turtle's face suddenly appeared out of nowhere an inch from her nose! It stuck its neck out and actually touched her nose. "Aaaaah!" Alex screamed, fell, and landed flat on her back in the grass.

"She kissed you! She really kissed you! Wow, she's never kissed anyone but me before." Jason hopped all around Alex in his excitement.

Alex lay still. The thought of kissing a turtle made her feel sick. Jason flopped down beside her.

"You know," he told her solemnly, "it's true. Clementine's never kissed anyone else before."

"Wonderful," Alex groaned.

"Alex! What are you doing down here? You're supposed to be up there." Barbara had returned and was pointing at the tree.

"Have you ever been kissed by a turtle before?" Alex asked her sister.

"Huh? Come on, Alex, quit goofing around. Here's the lantern for you to hang. . . . Oh, no! Jason! You squished a petunia."

Jason scrambled away from the tree. Barbara bent over and tried to straighten the flower. As soon as she let go of it, it dropped to the ground again.

"See what you did, Jason!" Barbara shouted angrily. "Yuck! Get that ugly creature out of here!" She pointed at Clementine.

Alex, no longer feeling sick, decided that the safest place to be was back up the tree. "Pppt! Tunia!" she sang as she climbed. She watched

Jason run out of the yard with Clementine. *Wonder where Homer is,* she thought.

"Here! Hang this up!" ordered Barbara as she held the lantern up for Alex to take.

"You could say 'please,' you know," Alex told her. She hung the lantern on a branch. Barbara stared at her. "You've been bossin' me and everyone else around all day," Alex added.

"Alex! The kids'll be here in a couple of hours. I have to get everything ready," Barbara exploded.

"Well, we've been helping you all day. At least you could appreciate it!" Alex yelled back.

"I do appreciate it!" hollered Barbara.

"Well, it doesn't seem like it!"

"Alex! This party is very important to me!"

"More important than your family's feelings? More important than Jason's feelings?" questioned Alex.

Barbara's face turned bright red. For a moment she wore a surprised expression. Then sparks of anger shone in her eyes. "Don't you talk to me like that!" she snapped at Alex. "What do you know anyway? You're just a dumb little kid."

"Oh, yeah?" cried Alex. "Then I'm too dumb and too little to hang up a lantern!" With that, Alex yanked the lantern off the branch and flung it down on the grass.

CLUNK! CLUNK! RATTLE! RATTLE! The lantern rolled across the yard. Barbara chased after it. Alex did a hurried skin-the-cat off the tree and ran inside and up the stairs to her room. She closed her door. That oughta teach Miss Mushy. What was the matter with her anyway?

Alex picked up her stuffed cat, Garfield, and hugged him. She and Garfield stomped around the room. "Teenagers! I don't ever want to be one," she told Garfield.

Alex wondered if she'd get in trouble for throwing the lantern on the ground. She climbed up on her bed and peeped out the window beside it. She could see her sister sitting on the patio below, holding the lantern in her hands. Barbara's head was bent over it.

"Why is she just sitting there?" Alex asked herself. "Maybe she's trying to figure out how to hang it in the tree. Miss Mushy never was very good at climbing trees. Why doesn't she get up and do something? She looks lonely and sorta sad. Brussels sprouts, maybe I shouldn't have thrown the lantern. Guess I lost my temper again . . . like with Alexandria."

Alex glanced at her clock radio. It was almost six o'clock. Miss Mushy's friends would be here in an hour and a half. It would take Miss Mushy that long to get dressed and curl her hair and paint her fingernails and do all the other goofy stuff that she did to get ready for a party! "Guess I better say I'm sorry and hang up the lantern. I don't want Miss Mushy to be sad for her party."

Just then a knock sounded at Alex's bedroom door. "Come in," she called. Barbara walked into the room. They stared at one another for a minute. "I'm sorry!" they cried at once. Immediately both sisters collapsed on the bed with giggles.

As soon as they could stop laughing, Barbara said, "Alex, you were right. I never thought about anyone's feelings but my own. This dumb party isn't as important as my family. I hope you'll forgive me."

"Aw, that's okay," answered Alex. "I

shouldn't have thrown your lantern out of the tree. I'll go hang it up right now!'' She started out the door. ''You better hurry up and get ready,'' she called over her shoulder. ''You only have an hour and a half to get dressed.''

Alex heard her sister's laugh ring through the house. Alex laughed, too. She skipped down the steps and out the back door.

The lantern was lying on its side under the tree. Alex picked it up. One side was a little dented and the candle was broken, but nothing else was damaged. She ran back inside, grabbed another candle from a drawer in the kitchen, and ran outside again. She stuck the candle in its holder and climbed the tree. Once more Alex hung the lantern on a tree limb. It was so peaceful up in the tree that Alex decided to stay there for a while. She settled her back against some branches and let her feet dangle.

''Isn't it funny that a few minutes ago, I was supermad at Miss Mushy and now I'm super-happy,'' she asked herself. ''It's almost like I've become a different person.'' Alex giggled again at remembering how she and Miss Mushy had said "I'm sorry" at the same time. Forgiveness! That's what had made everything change from sad to happy.

"What about Alexandria? Would forgiveness really work the same way with Alexandria? Can I forgive her after all the rotten things she's done to me? Blah!" Alex didn't want to think about that right now.

"Well, Firecracker," said a deep voice. "Are you taking a little snooze up there? Did Her Majesty work you too hard?"

Alex gazed down at her father standing under the tree with a volleyball net slung over his shoulder and his arms full of poles and stakes and a ball.

"Do you think I ought to wash this net in bleach so it will shine in the moonlight?" He winked at her.

"Can I help you set it up?" asked Alex eagerly.

"That would be much appreciated, Firecracker," answered her father as he set everything down on the patio.

"Catch me!" she yelled, standing up on a

limb. Father held out his arms. Alex pounded her chest, let out a Tarzan yell, and jumped into the air.

"Wow, you didn't move even one bit when I jumped on you," she told her father.

"That's what a father is—steady as a rock," he told her.

"Well, I'm glad you're not really a rock! I wouldn't want to cut myself on any of your sharp points."

"That's also what a father is, Firecracker . . . steady as a rock and gentle as a lamb."

Alex felt a sudden rush of love for her father. She hugged him hard and they both skipped off to set up the volleyball net.

CHAPTER 7

A Cookie Jar Message

SMACK! SMACK! SMACK! Paper airplanes hit everywhere! They hit the table, the stack of Bibles on the table, the crayon container, and the girls sitting around the table. One crashed into Alex's head.

The boys' side of the room erupted with ear-splitting whistles, sounds of bombs falling, and hilarious laughter.

"All right, girls, let's get 'em!" Each girl picked up an airplane or two and zoomed them back at the boys. Instantly, the room was in utter chaos. Airplanes flew, children chased, chairs fell, and tables scooted.

"HEY! TOWER TO PILOTS! TOWER TO PILOTS! OBSTRUCTION ON RUNWAY! FLIGHT PATTERNS IN ERROR! AWAIT IN-

STRUCTIONS!'' A loud voice rose above the noise and confusion in the Sunday school room. Pete, the owner of the voice, strode through the room catching airplanes in midair and rescuing those that had crashed.

The children laughed. They all took their seats and watched Pete eagerly to see what he would do next. *He's so much fun,* thought Alex. *Lisa's fun, too. I'm glad they're our teachers.*

The two teenagers, Pete and Lisa, had taken over the second-grade Sunday school class last spring when the regular teacher had moved away.

''Boy, I can't leave you guys for a minute,'' laughed Pete. ''Ah, Lisa to the rescue,'' he announced as a dark-haired young woman appeared in the doorway. Lisa walked over to Pete.

''What happened to you?'' she exclaimed, pointing to the mound of paper airplanes covering a table.

''Air raid!'' he answered. Giggles filled the room.

''Ahem! Okay, kids,'' Pete called. ''Let's tune in to Jesus and see what He's going to teach us today.'' He walked over to the closet and pulled a rather large object out of it. It was covered with a beach towel. He set it down on a table and wouldn't let anyone look under the towel.

"I wonder what that is," Alex whispered to the girl next to her.

"You'll all get to see what's under the towel in a few minutes," promised Lisa, "but first I want to ask you a question. Does anybody remember what parables are?"

"They're stories," cried one girl.

"That's right, Terri," Lisa said. "Parables are made-up stories that teach us how to live. Jesus told many parables that are in the Bible. One was about a man who owed a king ten million dollars. When the king asked the man to pay the money, the man fell down before the king and asked him to be patient. The man said he would pay it all. The king felt sorry for the man and forgave him. He said the man did not have to pay the ten million dollars.

"Then the man went to a second man who owed him two thousand dollars. When the first man asked the second man to pay him the two thousand dollars, the second man fell down before the first man and asked him to be patient. He promised to pay it all. But the first man got angry and had the second man thrown in jail.

"When the king heard about this, he got angry and told the first man that he should have forgiven the second man just as the king had forgiven him. The king sent the first man to the torture chamber until he had paid every penny of the ten million dollars."

There was a moment's silence after Lisa finished telling the story from the Bible. Alex sat uncomfortably on her chair. Forgiveness! Here was the same problem that she had been wrestling with for the last few days.

"Can anybody tell me why the king got so angry with the first man?" Lisa asked the class.

"He got mad because he forgave the first man, but the first man wouldn't forgive the second man," a girl named Stephanie answered.

"That's right," said Lisa. "What do you think this parable has to do with us? Jesus always told parables to teach us something. What does it teach us, Cara?"

"To forgive others!"

"Just like who, Cara?"

"The king!"

"Good! The king in this story was a forgiving king. Do we have a forgiving king in our lives?" Lisa asked.

"God!" the class responded.

"Has God forgiven us anything?"

"Our sins," answered Alex.

"Yes," said Linda, "and that's worth a lot more than ten million dollars, isn't it? You see, our Lord came down to earth and died for all of our sins—every wrong thing that we have done in the past or will do in the future. Since God forgave all of those sins, surely we can forgive each other's sins."

Lisa smiled at the class. "And now," she said, "let's see what mystery Pete has hidden under this beach towel."

Pete slowly began pulling off the towel. Squeals of excitement rippled through the classroom. As more of it was uncovered, Alex could see that it was something made of glass. It looked kind of like . . . a jar. A giant cookie jar! It even said so! Across the front of it, printed in big red

letters, was the word, COOKIES!

"Let's pretend that this is your cookie jar," Pete suggested to the class. "Is there anything sad about this cookie jar?"

"It's empty!" Alex immediately cried. Her stomach was beginning to rumble.

"Yep, this poor old jar has no cookies in it," Pete agreed. He waited for them all to stop moaning. "Okay, let's pretend that you have your best friend over—you know, the friend who plays with you and spends the night with you and eats cookies with you!

"You and your friend are hungry. Your friend says, 'May I have a cookie?' You say, 'Sure!' and you both run into the kitchen. But when you get there, the cookie jar is empty!

"Your friend is very disappointed. 'I always give you cookies at my house,' your friend says. You remember that you ate cookies at your friend's house yesterday. You feel like you owe your friend some cookies. But what can you do? The jar is empty.

"Suddenly, your father bursts through the door. 'Did I hear someone talk about cookies?' he asks. He's just come home from the grocery store. He's carrying a large sack like this one." Pete held up a grocery sack.

"Your father walks over to the cookie jar and opens the lid. He reaches into the sack and begins filling the jar with cookies!" Pete began pulling handfuls of cookies out of the sack and dropping them into the jar. The children's eyes grew wider and wider. Some smacked their lips or rubbed their stomachs.

"Your father fills up the whole jar! Now you have enough cookies for you and your friend to eat and a whole lot more left over.'' Pete gave them all a happy grin.

''This is how God passes His forgiveness to us. Think of the cookies as forgiveness. Just as you owed your friend cookies, you also owe people forgiveness. You need to forgive your brother or sister for playing with your toys without asking you. You need to forgive the kid at school who called you a bad name. You may even need to forgive your parents for blaming you for something you didn't do. But forgiving is hard work. Sometimes you may feel like you don't have any forgiveness inside of you to give to others. Your heart may feel like the cookie jar used to be—empty!

''Remember, your Heavenly Father knows when you feel empty. He passes His forgiveness to you. He fills you up just like the cookie jar was filled with cookies. Then, when you are filled with His forgiveness, you can pass some on to others. Whenever you feel that you can't forgive someone, just remember how much forgiveness your Father in Heaven gives to you. His Son, Jesus, died so that you would receive it. Use His forgiveness to share with others.

"And now," Pete cried in a louder voice, "LET'S EAT COOKIES! On your mark! Get set! Go!" He handed out cookies as fast as he could—right, left, right, left.

Alex sat quietly munching her cookies. She didn't talk or laugh with the other children. She was too busy thinking about Pete's story and the parable that Lisa had told.

Finally, after finishing her second cookie, Alex whispered, "Okay, Lord, I'll try to forgive Alexandria."

CHAPTER 8

French Fry Attack

The sun beamed sparkles of light through the trees. The flowers and grass caught the beams and shimmered brightly. Everything looked fresh and new. Monday morning! A new week! A new beginning!

Alex felt wonderful as she and Mother and Rudy drove to swim team practice. Forgiveness didn't seem so hard on such a beautiful morning.

All of Alex's wonderful feelings soon disappeared, however, at practice. For one thing, she was a few minutes late and had to scurry to a place in the back row to do the warm-up exercises. She tried giving Alexandria a friendly smile, but it was met with such an ugly look that Alex's own smile instantly disappeared.

Something else worried Alex. Several other

girls on the team surrounded her, telling her that they didn't like Alexandria either and that they were on "Alex's side." Soon the girls on the team split into two groups. One group stuck with Alexandria and the other with Alex! The battle between two girls was now a battle between two groups of girls.

To make matters worse, the girls around Alex kept the bad feelings strong by reminding each other how horribly Alexandria and her friends behaved.

"I heard Alexandria say that you're just a crybaby," Shellie told Alex.

"She also said you're a rotten swimmer!" shouted Laura.

"And that you must think you're a boy 'cause your name is Alex," added Amy.

Alex's cheeks burned and her eyes flashed with anger. How dare anyone call her a crybaby or a rotten swimmer! "I do not think I'm a boy!" Alex snapped.

"Let's dump her in the water," one of the girls suggested.

"Yeah, come on, Alex, we gotta get her back

for saying those things about you.''

''Hey! Watch out!'' Alex ducked. A rock whizzed over her head and crashed into the fence behind her. No one knew for sure who had thrown the rock, but from its direction it seemed likely to have come from Alexandria's side of the pool.

''I HAVE HAD ENOUGH!'' hollered Coach Bob suddenly. ''Everyone, into the water! Shallow end!''

The swimmers all jumped in quickly. Coach Bob stood above them at the edge of the pool. He was furious.

''Who threw that rock?'' he demanded. No one answered. ''I will not tolerate rock throwing or fighting or any violent actions on this team! If I see anyone hurting or trying to hurt anyone else, he or she will be kicked off the team immediately! Is that understood?'' Coach Bob looked directly at Alexandria and her group of friends and then he looked at Alex and her group of friends.

After a few moments, his face relaxed. ''Okay, team, let's warm up with some sprints. I want you to line up boy-girl-boy-girl across the length of the pool.

Boy-girl-boy-girl? The girls looked at each other and groaned. The boys looked at each other and made faces. *He's probably trying to break up the girls,* Alex guessed. What a mess! Everything was getting too far out of control. The forgiveness lesson by Pete and Lisa seemed unreal and far away . . . as if it existed in another world . . . a peaceful world, not at all like this one. Even the Lord seemed far away.

The whistle blew. Alex dove and swam as hard and as fast as she could. Once again, she was going to try to swim away all her troubles.

"Well, can we get a hot dog now?" Alex asked her sister a third time. Barbara opened one eye and squinted at Alex. She sat up, looked at the clock, lay back down, and mumbled, "We'll go to the snack bar in fifteen minutes!"

Alex sighed. How could Miss Mushy stand to lie in the hot sun all day covered with that oily junk? Alex noticed a gnat flying around her sister's foot. It landed and stuck on one of Barbara's toes. *Just like a tar pit,* thought Alex. She reached over to try and rescue the gnat.

"Alex! Quit tickling!"

"I'm just getting a bug off you!"

"What?" Barbara shrieked and sat up quickly.

"It's just a gnat," explained Alex. "See?"

"Oh, good grief! Go swim or something till lunchtime." Barbara sank back down in her chair.

"I'm starving," grumbled Alex. She walked a few steps and jumped into the pool. She wasn't going to swim. She was going to stand in the water and watch the clock. Miss Mushy was not going to get away with more than fifteen minutes.

Suddenly, loud laughter sounded from one side of the pool. Alex turned and looked behind her. Brussels sprouts! Not far from her were several girls sitting in a circle. They were laughing and shouting at one another while playing some kind of game. Alexandria was among them.

Maybe they won't see me, Alex hoped. She quickly ducked underwater and stayed there, coming up only for a second now and then to catch a breath of air.

It was during one of those seconds that Alex

thought she heard someone calling her name. She immediately ducked again. Alexandria and her friends must be yelling at her!

Alex stayed underwater until she had to come up for air again. She quickly ducked back under the water, but now she was certain someone was calling her name. Could it be Miss Mushy? Alex decided she'd better find out.

"ALEX!"

Alex wiped the water out of her eyes and blinked up at her sister standing on the concrete above her. Miss Mushy had been screaming her name so loudly that surely Alexandria and her friends knew she was here. Alex stole a quick glance at the circle of girls. They were all staring at her.

"What do you want?" Alex hissed at Barbara.

"What do you mean what do I want? I thought you were starving to death," her sister snapped. "Come on, let's eat lunch."

"Oh," was all Alex replied. She could feel hatred stares stabbing her all over as she climbed out of the pool.

"Are you okay? You don't look so good,"

said Barbara.

"Let's get outa here," Alex whispered. She grabbed her towel, whipped it around her shoulders, and quickly headed for the snack bar. Barbara followed, shaking her head in puzzlement.

Standing in line, catching tantalizing whiffs of food, made Alex feel better. She remembered how hungry she was. She wished she could run up to the front of the line, but that wouldn't be right.

"Alex!" a chorus of sickly sweet voices sang behind her.

Alex did not turn around. She knew to whom those voices belonged. She decided to ignore them.

"Alex, some of your friends must be in line. Didn't you hear them calling you?" Barbara asked her.

"They are not my friends!" retorted Alex. She didn't look at Barbara. She didn't look at anyone. She could feel her face turning red.

"Alex!" the voices called again. "Don't you want to talk to us, Alex?"

Alex clenched her fists and stared straight

ahead. Only two more people were ahead of her in line. *Hurry up,* she thought impatiently.

A woman at the counter was ordering hamburgers for herself and five children. "Now, Susie wanted one with cheese, and Billy, what did you want? Oh, yes, everything on it but pickles, and we need, let's see, two plain hamburgers, and one . . ."

"Come on," grumbled Alex. She heard giggles behind her—not the funny kind of giggles but the mean kind. She felt Barbara stir uncomfortably beside her.

The woman with the five children slowly left the counter. The only person now ahead of Alex was a small boy.

"I wanna ice-cream cone," he said to the teenage boy behind the counter.

"What flavor?" the older boy sighed tiredly.

"Strawberry!"

"We don't have strawberry—only chocolate or vanilla."

"I want strawberry!" the little boy demanded.

"Hey, look, chocolate or vanilla—that's all we've got."

"No!" The little boy folded his arms tight across his chest.

"Look, kid," the teenager behind the counter growled, "there's no strawberry! Now if you don't want chocolate or vanilla, get out of line and let somebody else have a turn." He motioned for Alex to step up to the counter.

As soon as Alex began ordering cheeseburgers and french fries for Barbara and herself, the little boy shrieked and burst into tears. "Waaaaaa! Mommy! They won't gimme my ice cream!"

"What's the matter? What's going on here, Tommy?" A large woman in a bright-flowered bathing suit suddenly appeared at Alex's right side. Her voice shouted in Alex's right ear.

"He won't gimme my ice cream, and she cut in line in front of me!" The little boy pointed at the boy behind the counter and then at Alex.

The woman frowned and pushed herself in front of Alex. "Young man, would you kindly get my son an ice-cream cone?"

"Chocolate or vanilla?" sighed the older boy.

"What flavor do you want, Tommy?" asked his mother.

''Chocolate,'' replied Tommy, smiling sweetly at his mother.

Shrugging his shoulders and shaking his head, the teenager handed a chocolate ice-cream cone to the woman. She passed the cone to her son and patted his head. Turning to Alex she said, ''You should be ashamed of yourself for shoving in front of a little boy like that!''

Before Alex could reply, the woman grabbed her son's hand and pulled him to a table.

Alex leaned on the counter with both hands under her chin. It upset her when grown-ups treated children unfairly. ''Brussels sprouts! They're suppose to set good examples for us kids,'' she exclaimed to herself.

''A-l-e-x!'' called a voice behind her.

''Aren't you ashamed, A-l-e-x?'' called another voice.

''Cutting in front of a little boy, tsk, tsk, tsk!'' That voice was Alexandria's.

Alex began to shake with anger. There were too many people treating her unfairly!

''Two cheeseburgers, two fries, two Cokes!'' shouted the boy behind the counter. He slapped the food and drinks down in front of Alex.

Barbara handed the boy some money while Alex furiously slammed the food onto a tray and slopped ketchup all over her french fries. Alex grabbed the food tray and turned to look for an empty table. She saw one in the corner and started toward it. Barbara picked up their Cokes and began to follow Alex.

Alex had to walk past Alexandria and her friends to get to the table. She knew she shouldn't look at Alexandria, but something made Alex look at her anyway. A smart-aleck grin spread across Alexandria's face.

An overpowering desire to shatter that grin took hold of Alex. Before she realized what she was doing, she snatched up her french fry container and flung it at the grin!

"Oh! Yuck! Ooooh! Blaaaa!" screamed Alexandria. Fries and ketchup dripped down Alexandria's face onto her shoulders. Parts of her blonde hair oozed red.

Alex stared at Alexandria in horror. Had she really done that? After a shocked silence, everyone began hollering.

"Alex!" shrieked Barbara.

"Disgusting!" howled Alexandria's friends.

"Hey, kid!" yelled the teenage boy behind the counter.

Alex didn't wait to hear anymore. She dropped the tray on the cement, splattering the rest of the food over everyone's feet, and ran out of the snack area as fast as she could.

Past the pool, out the gate, and down the driveway Alex dashed. She slowed down only an instant to yank her bicycle out of the rack. Pedalling furiously, Alex sped down the sidewalk and into the street. She didn't know whether to turn right or left. She only knew she had to get out of there fast!

CHAPTER 9

Forgiveness at Last

Alex wobbled to a stop in front of a large, two-story house. *Another dead-end street! I bet I've ridden down a hundred dead-end streets today . . . and they've all ended in circles!*

Ever since her escape from the pool, Alex had raced up, down, and around street after street. Her thoughts had flown as fast as her pedals. She felt angry, guilty, and sad all at the same time.

It's all Alexandria's fault, she told herself. *Alexandria and her friends are mean! She deserved to get french fries thrown in her face! Still, I did a really bad thing today. I keep doing worse and worse things. I must be turning into a bad person. Everything's going wrong!*

"Brussels sprouts," moaned Alex. She let her

bicycle fall to the ground, half in the street and half on the sidewalk that ran in front of the big, two-story house.

Alex plopped to the ground beside her bike. She scrunched down further and further until she lay with her head on the grass, her back on the sidewalk, and her feet stuck out in the street.

What am I going to do? I don't know where I am. I can't find my way home. Mom and Dad are gonna be mad when Miss Mushy tells them what I did and they'll be extra mad when they find out I left the pool by myself!

Alex stared up at the sky. She stared for a long time. Wispy clouds drifted around the sky. Birds flew by and sang their songs. Leaves waved gently in the trees. The sun shone brightly. Everything seemed peaceful up there.

"Well, it's sure a mess down here," sighed Alex. "I wish I were a bird or a tree or even a cloud. If I were a cloud I could glide across the whole sky! I'd see lots of different places—jungles and oceans and mountains. I could sit right on top of a mountain! And airplanes would fly through me . . . and if I didn't like somebody,

I'd rain on 'em! I'd pour a whole thunderstorm on Alexandria!

"I started out this morning all ready to forgive Alexandria," Alex moaned bitterly. "But then . . . oh, I don't know what happened! I just can't do it! I give up!"

It was then that Alex recalled Pete's story about the cookie jar and that, just like a cookie jar is filled up with cookies, God fills His children up with forgiveness so that they can pass that forgiveness on to others.

Alex lay perfectly still in the grass. "Okay, okay, I'll try it! I'll ask God!" she told the clouds. "Heavenly Father," she prayed, "please fill me up with forgiveness like the cookie jar." She paused a moment. Tears began rolling down her cheeks. "I can't forgive Alexandria by myself. I really need Your help."

There! She had done all she could. It was up to God now. The tears stopped. Feeling more relaxed and peaceful but very tired, Alex's eyes began to close. She thought she was still staring at the clouds in the sky, but they were the clouds in her dreams. Alex fell fast asleep.

"WHAT ARE YOU DOING SLEEPING ON MY GRASS?"

Alex's dreams burst! Her eyes popped open! She blocked the sun with one hand and squinted at a shape towering above her. Was that Alexandria?

"Huh?" squeaked Alex.

"I SAID, WHAT ARE YOU DOING SLEEPING ON MY GRASS?"

My grass? What does she mean "my grass"? And what's Alexandria doing here, anyway? Alex's head ached and she was terribly thirsty.

"I OUGHTA CLOBBER YOU!" shouted Alexandria.

"Oh . . . yeah," Alex mumbled. She couldn't think clearly. Her mind moved in slow motion. It was so hot! Was she awake or was she still dreaming? Alex started to sit up but felt so dizzy that she lay back down again. If only somebody'd give her a drink.

"What's the matter with you?" Alexandria demanded?

"Water!" gasped Alex, like a dying cowboy lost in the desert. "Please, water!"

She must have worried Alexandria, who quickly ran away and came back again with a tall glass of ice water. She set the glass on the grass beside Alex with a puzzled expression on her face.

Alex raised herself on one elbow and shakily gulped down the water, spilling part of it down her neck. She collapsed on her back again and began to moan, "It's so hot! I'm so hot!"

"Well, why don't you get out of the sun?" Alexandria cried.

Alex didn't answer. She stayed where she was and only moaned and groaned softly. This was too much for Alexandria.

She grabbed Alex's arms and dragged her across the lawn and under a shade tree. She then leaped to a row of bushes along the front of the house, pulled a garden hose out from under them, aimed it at Alex, and turned the water on full blast.

"Ahhhhhhhh!" shrieked Alex and leaped to her feet. Alexandria made sure Alex was thoroughly drenched before turning the water off.

"What'd you do that for?" Alex spluttered.

"I was cooling you off!" Alexandria looked

relieved to see that Alex had recovered from her "heat stroke."

"Well, did you have to spray me in the face?" cried Alex.

"What are you bellyaching about?" shouted Alexandria. "I only put water in your face! You put a lot more than water in my face!"

"Oh. . . ." Alex dug her toe into the ground and glanced sideways at Alexandria. "I guess water's better'n french fries—thrown in your face, I mean." She sat back down under the tree.

"You're not gonna lie down and act weird again, are you?" asked Alexandria coming up to stand beside her.

"No," replied Alex.

"Well, then, what are you doing here?" asked Alexandria.

"I'm lost!"

"Oh."

"What are *you* doing here?" Alex asked Alexandria.

"Me?" Alexandria exclaimed. "I live here!"

"You do?" Alex was amazed. That meant she had been sleeping in Alexandria's front yard!

How did that happen? She had ridden up many streets and passed many houses. Why did she stop at Alexandria's house? "Of course!" Alex suddenly exclaimed.

"Of course what?"

"I think God brought me to your house! You see, I've been praying that all this fighting between you and me would stop and that God would help me to forgive you and . . ."

"You forgive me?" Alexandria roared. "What about me forgiving you? You're the one who smeared me with french fries!"

"Well, you're the one who stood behind me in line and made fun of me!"

"Well, you're the one who knocked me into the pool and pulled my hair!"

"After you hung my goggles on top of the fence!"

"Well, you're the one—"

Both girls had started to yell the same thing at the same time. They stopped and eyed each other for a moment.

"You're the—"

It happened again! They had shouted the exact

same words. They gave each other puzzled looks.

"What's going on?"

The third time that it happened, Alex and Alexandria broke into shy giggles. The giggles got louder and louder until both girls were laughing hilariously. They rolled over the grass, laughing and holding their sides. And as they rolled, it seemed as if their quarrels also rolled away. The laughter healed their anger just as a soothing ointment heals a burn or a cut.

Later, with much panting and struggling for air, the two girls lay still. Alex felt that her stomach would never be the same again.

"Oh, I don't think I can move," groaned Alexandria.

With real effort, Alex sat up. She brushed the tears out of her eyes and off her cheeks and looked at Alexandria. Her face was also wet with tears.

"You know, that's funny!" Alex exclaimed.

"Oh, please, don't say anything more that's funny," begged Alexandria.

"No, I don't mean *funny* funny. I mean sorta *strange* funny."

"What?"

"Well, my mom says that a lot of times crying tears makes you feel better, and I was just thinking that it must be true for laughing tears, too!"

Alexandria gazed at Alex. "I think you're right," she agreed. She paused and then asked, "Do you really think God made you come to my house?"

"Sure! It wasn't my idea. I would have been afraid to go to your house, especially after what I did to you today."

"Hmmm. Maybe you're right."

"Uh, Alexandria?"

"Yeah?"

"I'm sorry for all the bad stuff I've done."

"Oh," Alexandria shrugged, "that's okay and I'm sorry, too."

"That's okay!" Alex quickly replied. *Brussels sprouts! We've both forgiven each other,* Alex thought, *and it was really kinda easy!*

Suddenly, a voice called from the door of the house, "Alexandria! Time for dinner!"

"Coming!" Alexandria shouted. She motioned for Alex to follow her. "Come on, Alex. You can call your parents to come and get you."

"My parents!" Alex exclaimed. She'd forgotten about them. They must be really worried. And what about Miss Mushy? She'd left her at the swimming pool a long time ago. "I suppose I'll be in gobs of trouble when I get home," she muttered as she followed Alexandria into the house.

CHAPTER 10

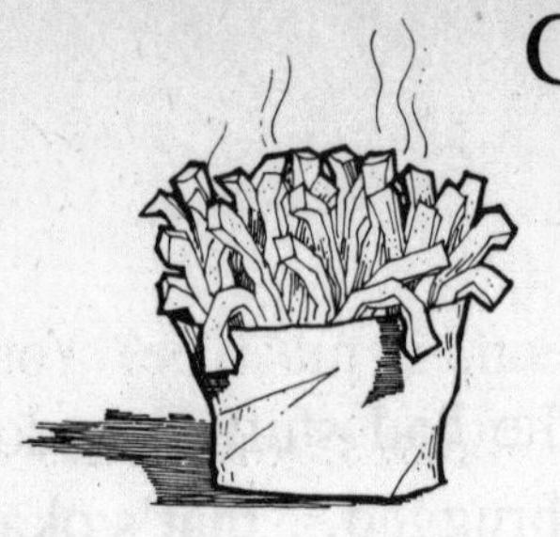

Friends

Alexandria led the way through her house and into the kitchen. A tall, blonde-haired woman was busy scooping french fries into a basket. Alex and Alexandria took one look at the french fries and began to giggle.

"Mom," Alexandria said between giggles, "this is Alex."

"Why, hello, Alex," her mother responded with a surprised look. "Do you mean Alex from the swimming team?" she asked Alexandria.

"Yes, Mom, we're friends now."

"That's good," her mother smiled. "Where do you live, Alex?"

"On Juniper Street," Alex replied in her most polite voice.

"Juniper Street? That is quite a ways from

our house."

"Yes, I know. I mean, it must be. You see, I'm lost. I should have been home hours ago," Alex told her.

"My goodness!" Alexandria's mother exclaimed. "You had better call your parents right away."

"You can call them from my room," Alexandria told her. "Come on."

"Alexandria, hurry up and come back downstairs," her mother called after them. "Your father's bringing the hamburgers in from the grill right away. Oh, and Alex, you might as well eat a hamburger with us."

Alex followed Alexandria up some stairs and into her bedroom. Alex gasped in delight. Garfield posters covered the walls. "Do you like Garfield, too?" Alex cried. "He's my favorite animal in the whole world."

"Mine, too," agreed Alexandria. "Well, except for Elizabeth, of course."

"Who's Elizabeth?" Alex wanted to know.

"My cat. See, she's right there on the bed." Alexandria pointed. "She likes to hang out with the stuffed animals, so I guess she kind of blends in with them."

"Oh," Alex breathed. She got down on her knees and began to stroke Elizabeth's back. "She's purring," Alex cried in delight. "I wish we had a cat."

"And I wish I had a big sister like yours," Alexandria said.

"You do?" Alex looked surprised.

"Yeah, she really stood up for you today at the pool," Alexandria told her.

"She did?"

"You should have heard her," Alexandria replied. "She said that you had never thrown french fries in anybody's face before and that you must have been really upset to do such a thing. And she said that I must have done something to hurt you to make you so upset."

"Really? She really said all that?" Alex exclaimed.

"Yeah, and she also said that if we kept on fighting, we might really hurt each other." Alexandria paused and then said, "You know, you ought to be glad you have a sister like that."

Alex let out a long whistle. "Brussels sprouts," she muttered. It was neat to know that Miss Mushy had stood up for her.

"Hey! You have to call your parents," Alexandria suddenly remembered.

"Yeah, I better," Alex agreed. "Where's the telephone?"

"Right there," Alexandria pointed beside her bed.

Alex found the telephone and smiled. It was lavender, just like Alexandria's swimming suit.

With a sigh, Alex picked up the phone and dialed her home number. She hoped her parents would not be too angry with her.

"Hello?" her mother answered the telephone.

"Uh, hi, Mom," Alex stammered.

"Alex! Where have you been? Where are you? Are you all right?" Mother cried.

"Yes, Mom, I'm okay. I'm sorry I've been gone so long. I didn't mean to be. I got sort of lost. Could you come and get me?"

"Of course I will come and get you," Mother replied. "Where are you?"

"You won't believe this, Mom," Alex warned

her. "I am at Alexandria's house!"

"What?" Mother exclaimed. "Alexandria? Not the one you threw french fries at today?"

"Uh, yeah, the same one," Alex admitted. "I guess Barbara told you all about it."

"Yes, she did," replied Mother. "It sounded awful. But, Alex, what are you doing at Alexandria's house? Are you sure you are all right?"

"Yeah, Mom, we're friends now." Alex told her mother all that had happened since she left the pool.

By the end of the story, Mother was laughing. "Wait until I tell your father and your sister," she chuckled. "You are right. It is hard to believe."

Alex could hear Barbara in the background asking, "Tell me what?" Rudy was yelling, "Me, too! Tell me, too!"

"Alex," Mother said. "Give me Alexandria's address, and we will pick you up as soon as your father comes home. He is out right now looking for you."

"Oh, no," Alex groaned.

"We have been awfully worried about you,"

Mother said. "We were about ready to call the police."

"I'm sorry," Alex said meekly.

"That's okay, just give me the address."

Alex asked Alexandria her address and repeated it to Mother. Then she asked, "Mom, is it okay if I eat dinner here? They are having hamburgers and french fries."

Mother laughed again and told Alex she could. She hung up the phone.

Just then a voice called from downstairs. "ALEXANDRIA!"

"Dinner must be ready," cried Alexandria. "Let's eat!"

"I can hardly wait!" Alex exclaimed, running down the stairway after Alexandria. "I didn't have lunch, you know."

"Yeah, I know," Alexandria giggled over her shoulder. "I had your lunch in my face!"

Alex made up for missing lunch by eating two hamburgers, a salad, and a double helping of french fries.

"Mmmm, that was really good! Thank you for dinner," Alex said.

"You're quite welcome, Alex," replied Alexandria's mother. "There are a few french fries left. Why don't you finish them up?"

Alex glanced at Alexandria. Both girls giggled.

"Why is it that every time I mention french fries you girls laugh? Is there something wrong with them?"

"Oh no, Mom," replied Alexandria. She winked at Alex.

Alex winked back and grinned. She and Alexandria had shared their french fry joke all through dinner. Instead of telling her family how Alex had thrown french fries at her, Alexandria had turned it all into a funny secret between them. By doing so, she had let Alex know that she was completely forgiven and Alex, in turn, felt true forgiveness in her heart for Alexandria. A warm, loving feeling steadily grew inside Alex. She was sure now that she and Alexandria were going to be friends—maybe even good friends!

"There's a car in the driveway," announced Alexandria's father.

"Oh, that must be for me." Alex jumped up from the table. "Excuse me!" she gasped and bounded out the front door. She collided with her parents on the front steps. Almost before she knew what had happened, Alex was swooped up into a double hug. Her mother and father grabbed her at the same time and neither let go.

"We're so glad to see you, Firecracker!"

"Thank God, you're safe!"

"We love you, Alex!"

Alex rested in her parents arms and let their whispers soak her mind with love. She felt that she could stay there forever. It was funny how she hadn't really missed her parents this afternoon, but now that she was with them, she never wanted to leave them again.

That special moment was over all too soon. Alexandria and her parents came outside and soon the grown-ups were introducing themselves. Alexandria grinned at Alex. "Boy! Everybody on the swim team will sure be surprised when we show up as friends!" she exclaimed.

"Well, that's the way it should be," said Alex. "After all, we're *two* Alexandrias!"

"Come on, Firecracker. I have your bike all loaded up. We better go now," her father called.

Alex ran to the car where Rudy and Barbara were waiting. She waved and shouted good-bye to Alexandria until the car turned the corner.

"Well!" exclaimed Barbara. "I'm not sure if that was the same Alexandria!"

"What do you mean?" questioned Alex.

"I mean, the Alexandria I saw this afternoon was mean and had a big scowl on her face and a loud mouth! This girl hardly seemed like the same person." Barbara leaned toward Alex. "Also, I noticed another big difference."

"What?"

"This Alexandria didn't have ooey, gooey ketchup and french fries dripping down her hair."

Alex pretended to punch her sister while the family laughed. When everyone quieted down, Alex told them all about being lost and being found and making friends with her enemy.

"You mean you were really sleeping in Alexandria's front yard?" Barbara asked. "I can't believe it!"

"Yeah, that was pretty incredible," agreed Alex, "but like I told Alexandria, I think that was God's idea. It sure wasn't mine!"

"I agree with you, Alex," said Mother. "Only the Lord could have arranged for you to end up at Alexandria's house."

"Yeah, He must have wanted us to stop fighting real fast," decided Alex.

"You're right, Firecracker," Father boomed from the front seat. "After all, who knows what you'd have used next time to smear in Alexandria's hair—mustard, pickles, pork and beans?"

"Oh, Dad, yuck!" cried Alex. The rest of them laughed.

When they reached home, everyone went inside but Alex. She lingered on the front porch. The air felt cooler and the sky was just beginning to darken. Alex remembered that sometime today—it seemed like ages ago—she had wanted to be a cloud and sail far away.

"I don't want to sail away anymore, Lord," she whispered. "Thank You, Father. Thank You for making everything so good again!"

A thrill of joy passed through Alex. Tomorrow would be a special day! She would go to swim team practice and Alexandria would be her friend. "It's going to be a great summer!" she shouted to the clouds and skipped into the house.

Amen.

SHOELACES AND BRUSSELS SPROUTS

One little lie, but BIG trouble!

When Alex lies to her mom about losing her shoelaces, it doesn't seem like a big deal. But how do you replace special baseball laces when you don't have any money and you're not allowed to go to the store alone? A big softball game is coming up, and Alex knows the coach won't let her pitch in shoes without laces—or in cowboy boots!

Every kid gets into the predicaments that Alex does—ones that start out small and mushroom. Readers will learn from Alex's mistakes and understand that they have the same sources of help that she turns to: A God who loves them and wants to help them, and parents who understand.

Other books in the Alex Series . . .

2 *French Fry Forgiveness*—Sometimes making friends is harder than making enemies.

3 *Hot Chocolate Friendship*—Is winning first place as important to Alex as being a friend?

4 *Peanut Butter and Jelly Secrets*—Obeying her parents (even in little things) beats the awful results of disobeying.

NANCY LEVENE, who shares Alex's love of softball, lives with her husband and daughter in Kansas.

HOT CHOCOLATE FRIENDSHIP

The worst possible partner!

That's who Alex gets for the biggest project of the school year. She won't have a chance at first place if she has to work with Eric Linden. He's the slowest kid in third grade.

Alex can't understand why he has to be her partner. Is she supposed to share God's love with Eric? Could that be more important than winning first place?

Every kid gets into the predicaments that Alex does—ones that start out small and mushroom. Readers will learn from Alex's mistakes and understand that they have the same sources of help that she turns to: A God who loves them and wants to help them, and parents who understand.

Other books in the Alex Series . . .

1 *Shoelaces and Brussels Sprouts*—It's always better to tell the truth, as Alex learns the hard way.

2 *French Fry Forgiveness*—Sometimes making friends is harder than making enemies.

4 *Peanut Butter and Jelly Secrets*—Obeying her parents (even in little things) beats the awful results of disobeying.

NANCY LEVENE, who shares Alex's love of softball, lives with her husband and daughter in Kansas.

PEANUT BUTTER AND JELLY SECRETS

Where did her money go?

Alex's mom *trusted* her with her school lunch money—and now it's gone! How will she ever get through the week without Mom *or* her teacher finding out? And what will she do when her class goes to lunch for the next five days?

Every kid gets into the predicaments that Alex does—ones that start out small and mushroom. Readers will learn from Alex's mistakes and understand that they have the same sources of help that she turns to: A God who loves them and wants to help them, and parents who understand.

Other books in the Alex Series . . .

1 *Shoelaces and Brussels Sprouts*—It's always better to tell the truth, as Alex learns the hard way.

2 *French Fry Forgiveness*—Sometimes making friends is harder than making enemies.

3 *Hot Chocolate Friendship*—Is winning first place as important to Alex as being a friend?

NANCY LEVENE, who shares Alex's love of softball, lives with her husband and daughter in Kansas.

THE KIDS FROM APPLE STREET CHURCH

How did it happen?

Every day brings new excitement in the lives of Mary Jo, Danny, and the other kids from Apple Street Church. Whether it's finding a stolen doll in a coat sleeve, chasing important papers all over the school yard, meeting a famous astronaut, or discovering the real truth about a mysteriously broken leg, the kids write it all in their personal notebooks to God.

Usually diaries are private. But this is your chance to look over the shoulders of The Kids from Apple Street Church as they tell God about their secret thoughts, their problems, and their fun times. It's just like praying, except they are writing to God instead of talking to Him.

Don't miss any of the adventures of The Kids from Apple Street Church!

1. Mary Jo Bennett
2. Danny Petrowski
3. Julie Chang
4. Pug McConnell
5. Becky Garcia
6. Curtis Anderson

ELSPETH CAMPBELL MURPHY has also written the popular God's Word in My Heart and David and I Talk to God series.